BEWARE!
DO NOT READ THIS
BOOK FROM
BEGINNING T

D1494913

Welcome to the Carnival of
ordinary carnival. Here y
rides. Exciting games of chance. And the weirdest Freak Show ever.

Do you dare to enter?

Are you brave enough to risk the Supersonic
Space Coaster? Will you know whom to trust—
the Snake Lady or the Three-headed Man? Can
you make it through the House of Horrors alive?

This scary adventure is all about *you*. You're
in control. You decide what will happen. And
you decide how terrifying the scares will be.

Start on page 1. Then follow the instructions
at the bottom of each page. You make the
choices.

If you make the right choices, you'll escape
from the spine-tingling Carnival of Horrors in
time. If you make the wrong choice ...
BEWARE!

So take a long, deep breath, cross your fingers,
and turn to page 1 to GIVE YOURSELF
GOOSEBUMPS!

READER BEWARE —
YOU CHOOSE THE SCARE!

Look for more
GIVE YOURSELF GOOSEBUMPS adventures
coming soon
from R.L. STINE

Give Yourself Goosebumps

Escape From the Carnival of Horrors

R.L. Stine

Hippo

Scholastic Children's Books,
Commonwealth House, 1–19 New Oxford Street, London WC1A 1NU
a division of Scholastic Ltd
London – New York – Toronto – Sydney – Auckland

First published in the USA by Scholastic Inc., 1995
First published in the UK by Scholastic Ltd, 1996

ISBN 0 590 13752 2

Typeset by Rowland Phototypesetting Ltd
Bury St Edmunds, Suffolk
Printed in China

10 9 8 7 6 5 4 3 2 1

"What do *you* want to do?"

"I don't know, Patty. What do *you* want to do?"

"Not fair, Brad. I asked you first."

Patty and Brad. Your two best friends. Arguing. As usual.

It's the last week of August. And Patty and Brad haven't stopped fighting since your summer holiday started.

Patty likes being bossy. You don't mind, though. It's no big deal.

It's hard to win a fight with her anyway. You don't know why Brad even tries. You guess it's because he doesn't want to look like a wimp in front of a girl.

"There's nothing to do. I guess I'll just go home," Brad says. He shoves his hands in his pockets. Then his shoulders slump and he sort of shrivels up. You guess Brad is a bit of a wimp—even if he is your best friend.

"You're so boring, Brad," Patty complains. Whenever Patty complains, her freckles really pop out. Now there are about a million of them spread across her face.

"Hey! I know what we should do!" Patty suddenly bursts out.

Go to PAGE 2.

2

"Let's bike over to Bennet's Field and watch them set up the carnival!"

"I don't know," you answer. "It's getting dark and Mum said I have to be in by nine."

"It's only a quick bike ride," Brad says. "Are you some kind of wimp?"

Brad calling you a wimp? You can't believe it!

"Okay. Okay," you agree. "But if it's as bad as last year, there won't be much to see. Don't you remember the main attraction?" you remind them. "The ride they called Terror Track? It turned out to be a baby choo-choo train that circled round and round and round."

It doesn't matter what you say. Patty's made up her mind. You're going to ride over to the carnival.

A hot, humid breeze blows in your face as you pedal along. Patty's in the lead. No surprise. And Brad's puffing behind you.

It's dark by the time you reach Bennet's Field.

You and your friends drop your bikes in the grass and race across the moonlit field, towards the huge wooden fence that surrounds the carnival.

To take a closer look, turn to PAGE 3.

As you reach the carnival entrance, you hear music coming from inside. Not the usual corny organ stuff they always play. But some really strange music. It sounds familiar and totally new at the same time.

Brad stretches his neck to try to peer over the fence. But no luck. The fence is far too high.

Patty jiggles the padlock on the door. It's sealed shut.

"I guess we'll have to wait until tomorrow night when the carnival opens," Brad says.

"No way," Patty says. "Let's climb the fence. Now!"

"Are you crazy?" Brad says. "We'll get caught!"

"Come on. There's probably no one in there," Patty replies.

Your friends turn to you to cast the deciding vote. You glance at your watch. It's almost 9:00 p.m. If you're going to get home in time, you should start back now.

What are you going to do?

If you decide to go home, turn to PAGE 10.

If you climb the fence to get inside, turn to PAGE 6.

"Wh-what do you mean?" Brad asks, trembling all over.

"I've just had an idea. A great idea," the man replies. "I want you kids to stay and try out the rides before the grand opening tomorrow."

Patty's eyes open wide. "Cool!" she says.

"Are you sure it's all right with the owner?" you ask.

"I'm Big Al, the manager. And what I say around here goes."

Big Al digs around in his checked jacket and pulls out three maps. He hands one to each of you.

"Study them carefully," he says. "If you have any questions, ask them now."

Your eyes fall upon the map. You have a question. But when you gaze up, Big Al is gone. He's vanished!

"A whole carnival to ourselves!" Patty exclaims. "Where should we start?"

You stare down at your map once again. You notice that the carnival is split in half. On one side are the rides. Tons of them. On the other side are the sidestalls, packed with games of chance and the Freak Show.

What will you try first?

To go on the rides, turn to PAGE 34.
To check out the sidestalls, turn to PAGE 77.

"Come on, run!" you yell to Patty and Brad as you spin around. "There's got to be another way out!"

Big Al blows a whistle. Its shrill blast hurts your ears. He blows it again and, suddenly, dozens and dozens of carnival people appear out of nowhere. But they don't look the way they did before.

Some have green flesh. Some are deathly white. Their rotting skin hangs from their bones. Above their sunken cheek-bones, their eyes glow an eerie yellow.

You watch in horror as more and more of them appear.

What should you do? Your legs won't budge. You can't think clearly. You're terrified! You stand there—frozen—in a trance.

But Brad breaks the spell when he screams out, "They're ghosts! That's why they're wearing those old-fashioned clothes. They're dead!"

"Watch out! Over there!" Patty yells. "That—that ghost . . . it's coming right at us. Run!"

Run to PAGE 127.

6

"Let's do it!' you say to your friends. "Let's climb the fence!"

Patty is halfway up before you finish speaking. You let Brad go next. You're last.

It's a hard climb up. There's really no place on the fence to get a good grip. But you make it to the top, swing your legs over, and tumble down. You land on the grass. You're inside!

You and your friends gaze around. It's pretty dark—the only light comes from torches. At first the carnival looks the same as it always does. Dinky rides. Hot dog wagons. Then the lights start to flicker on in every corner of the field— the rides start to move. It's as if the whole place is magically coming to life.

"Hey! Look at that giant roller coaster!" you exclaim, pointing up ahead. "They never had a roller coaster before!"

"Yeah," Brad agrees. "And the whole place is a lot bigger than last year!"

"This is awesome!" Patty says as she sprints towards the rides.

Race over to PAGE 7.

You and Brad take off after Patty. You all stop in front of the roller coaster.

"Wow!" Patty says as she gazes up at it. "It's like a rocket to outer space!"

Beyond the roller coaster, you spy a castle surrounded by a moat. And a spooky-looking haunted house sitting high atop a hill.

"These are the coolest rides I've ever seen!" you say. "They still have that stupid choo-choo train over there," you point out, "but we could ride this stuff all night and never go near it!"

Patty grabs your arm and tugs you over to the other side of the carnival—to the sidestalls. Brad races after you.

"Hey! Where are all those dinky wooden booths from last year?" you ask as you gawk at the amazing games of chance.

They're gone. And in their place are giant video games and huge spinning wheels studded with hundreds of blinking coloured lights!

"Get a load of that!" Brad suddenly cries out.

You and Patty spin around.

You can't believe what you see!

Be more amazed on PAGE 87.

8

You wander over to the Wheel of Chance and immediately notice two strange things.

First, you read the sign on the booth. It says Wheel of No Chance. Then you hear the barker's voice calling, "Step right up!" But there's no one there.

No one but a green-and-yellow parrot.

"Excuse me," you say, hoping someone will answer. "Is this game open?"

"No, I'm standing by this wheel for my health," the parrot cracks. "Now do you want to spin or what?"

The parrot is obviously annoyed. "Mammals," he mutters. "Can't live with them, can't live without them."

You steal a glance around. Maybe you should skip this game. But Big Al sneaks up behind you.

"Spin," he says. "You must earn enough points to win."

"But how will I know if I have enough points?" you ask.

"*Spin!*" It's his final word.

Go to PAGE 9.

Here's how to spin:

Close your eyes and twirl your finger over the wheel on this page. Then let your finger land somewhere on the wheel. Look at the number you've landed on. Go to that page next.

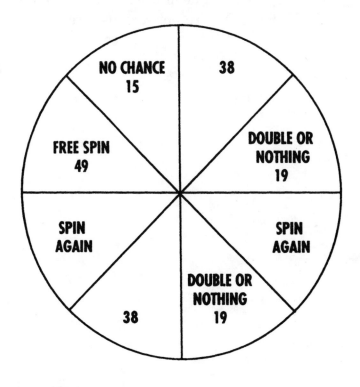

Quick! Go to the page you landed on!
       OR
If you landed on SPIN AGAIN, *spin again.*

10

You've decided not to sneak into the carnival? You're going home instead? Well, it's a good thing Patty usually makes all the decisions. Otherwise, you'd never have any fun! And this book would be over before it began!

Go ahead. Take a deep breath. Then go and climb the fence. You're not *scared*—are you?

Turn back to PAGE 6.

You've decided to help the freaks. As you race along, you spot Brad and Patty.

"Listen, guys," you tell them, lowering your voice. "We've got a problem. A big problem."

You take a deep breath and tell them all about Madame Zeno and the blue card.

"So," you finish saying, "somebody might need our help in the back of the Freak Show."

"What's a freak?" Brad asks nervously.

"Remember the poster we saw when we came in? The one with the three-headed man and the lady with the snake body?" you remind him.

Brad bites down on his lip. "Are they really real?"

"Sure they're real," Patty chimes in. "I once saw a bearded lady at the circus."

"I don't know," Brad says. "It sounds kind of creepy."

"Well, Madame Zeno said this was my fate. I'm going to help them—whatever they are. Are you guys in?"

"You bet," Patty answers, her eyes shining with excitement.

"Okay, okay. I'll go," Brad mumbles.

"Then let's hurry!" you exclaim.

Race to the back of the Freak Show on PAGE 35.

You run to the right. "Follow me!" you cry out to Patty and Brad.

You run faster than you've ever run in your life. Your sides ache, but you keep on going.

When your chest feels as if it's about to burst, you finally stop. And hear a crash behind you. Then at both sides of you. Then in front of you. Trapping you.

"Welcome to the Reptile's Petting Zoo," a deep voice echoes through the darkness.

Reptile's Petting Zoo? You thought the sign said *Reptile* Petting Zoo.

"Our alligator has been so lonely," the deep voice continues. "Waiting and waiting—for his new pets to arrive. And here you are—finally."

THE END

The room is dark, but all around you, you hear hushed moans. "Help us! Help us!"

"We're in a prison," Patty says. "And look at the prisoners! They're weird!"

Patty is right. As your eyes grow accustomed to the darkness, you see cell after cell. Each one holds a strange-looking prisoner. There's an enormous fat lady who's nearly bursting out of the bars. A giant. A dwarf. A young lady with boa constrictors wrapped around her waist. And a woman with a long black beard!

"We're the freakssss," the Snake Lady says. "Every night when the show ends, the master locks us up."

"The master? You mean Big Al is—" you start to say.

"You must help us!" the giant interrupts.

"Sssssssh," the Snake Lady says. "The master'sssss coming—you mustn't be here! Go! That way!" She points to a door down the hall.

Escape through the door down the hall, go to PAGE 48.

Stay and talk to Big Al, go to PAGE 62.

14

You reach out slowly and touch the red card.

To your amazement a 3-D heart magically appears and rises from the flat surface. Then it starts to beat! *Tha-dump, tha-dump*. It must be some fancy optical illusion. You lean closer to figure out the trick.

"Yowwwww!" you screech and jerk back to avoid the warm red liquid that nearly squirts in your eye. Is it blood? It looks like blood. "Wow! Cool effect," you say. "How did you do it?"

"Turn over the card," Madame Zeno orders. "Do it now!"

Madame Zeno really gets into her act. Doesn't she know this is just a game? you think. But you do as you're told.

Big deal. No weird pictures. No hidden fortunes. All you see are the numbers *1, 3, 2* shimmering in gold script against a midnight background. "What does it mean?" you ask.

"You will know when the time is right," the fortune-teller whispers. Her voice is so low, you can barely hear her. "It could save your life!"

What does she mean? Turn to PAGE 41 to find out.

Round and round the wheel spins. It finally lands on number *15*. NO CHANCE.

No chance. Does that mean what you think it means?

No chance at all.

Zip.

Zero.

Nothing.

Nada.

Negative.

Yes. That's exactly what it means. You have met . . .

THE END

16

"Hi!" you say to Big Al. "Who are all those people?"

He doesn't really answer your question.

"Welcome to the Carnival of Horrors," he says. "You *must* play or pay. We have many games here. You *must* play two." He practically spits the word *must* out. "If you succeed, you can win prizes. But if you lose, you pay with your life!"

Boy, he's really laying it on thick, you think. But it's a pretty cool gimmick. "Okay, I'll play a game. Then I've got to go home."

"No one goes home," Big Al says, "until they play. You must play *two* games. And survive."

"Okay. Okay," you mutter to yourself.

You glance around at the two closest games. Guess Your Weight on Mars and the Wheel of Chance. You have to pick one to start, or you'll never get out of here.

For Guess Your Weight on Mars, go to PAGE 72.

To play Wheel of Chance, go to PAGE 8.

You take a few steps along the way hoping you've won enough prizes and points. You notice the crowd of people surrounding Big Al. They're still chanting, "PAY OR PLAY. PAY OR PLAY."

You break through the crowd and grab Big Al's arm. "Hey! Do you know where my friends are?"

"Certainly," Big Al says, pointing up ahead. "They're right over there!"

"Patty! Brad!" you shout as you rush up to them. "Come on! We've got to go! This carnival is evil!"

But before they can say a word, Big Al's voice booms from behind you. "Not before The Final Challenge!"

The Final Challenge begins on PAGE 84.

18

The space lady slowly circles you as she sizes you up from head to toe. "Hmmmm, I think you weigh thirty-eight pounds."

"*Thirty-eight pounds!* Boy, are you wrong!"

"I'm never wrong," she says, smirking. She snaps her fingers and two enormous guards appear. They each take one of your arms and drag you out of the courtyard.

"I don't weigh thirty-eight pounds!" you yell. But then you remember. It isn't your weight on Earth that matters. It's your weight on Mars.

Do you weigh thirty-eight pounds on Mars? You'd better find out quickly, because something tells you that what Big Al said about having to survive *might* be true.

Weigh in on PAGE 134.

You land on number *19*.

"Double or nothing. Double or nothing," two voices behind you echo.

You whirl around—and gasp! It's a man with two heads.

"Congratulations. You win ten points," one head says to you. "Quit while you're ahead!"

"*Ahead*, get it? A head!" the other head adds, laughing hysterically.

"Shut up," head number one says.

"You shut up," head number two shoots back. "Ten points is nothing. You'd better spin again. And this time it's double or nothing. You get double the points wherever you land."

Which head should you listen to?

If you think you don't have enough points, go back to PAGE 9 and spin again.

If you think you have enough points and you haven't played Guess Your Weight, go to PAGE 72.

If you have played Guess Your Weight, go to PAGE 17.

It seems as if hours have passed. Or maybe it's only minutes.

You try to unclasp your hands. But they won't budge. It's as if your arms are glued around your knees.

You try to move something. Anything.

But you can't blink an eyelid. Your body is paralysed. You can't even scream.

A door opens and two men dressed in overalls and wearing gas masks amble in. Finally. They're here to rescue you!

"Looks like the perfume worked," you hear one of them say.

"Yeah. And just in time. We needed a new dummy for the Real-Life Space Display," the other adds.

They pick up your rigid body and carry you out. No wonder those astronauts in the silver tunnel looked so real!

Sorry. You can't scream. You can't escape.

Next time, you promise yourself, you'll stick with the baby rides. But then you remember—there isn't going to be a next time . . . because this is . . .

THE END

You're outside—standing in Bennet's Field—gazing at the fence that surrounds the carnival.

"I guess we'll have to wait until tomorrow night when the carnival opens," Brad says.

"No way," Patty says. "Let's climb the fence."

What's going on here?

You guessed it. The silver locker was a time machine. You've gone back in time to the first moment you spotted the carnival. Now it appears as if you have to start all over again—fighting horror after horror, right up to . . .

THE END

You're pretty sure that the space lady guessed wrong! Now all you have to do is step on the scales to prove it.

The two goons shove you inside the planet simulation chamber. It's a long narrow tube, and it's really stuffy inside. You can barely breathe.

You step up on the scales. You check the read-out. Boy, oh, boy! The space lady *is* wrong!

You jump up and down. "I won! I won!"

Back outside you collect your prize. It's a huge chocolate bar. You take a big bite out of it and stuff the rest in your pocket.

You gaze around. The coast is clear. Maybe you can find Patty and Brad and get out of here.

You walk a few steps forward. But a heavy hand clamps down on your shoulder from behind.

It's Big Al.

"It's time to play another game," he says, grinning.

If you have not tried the Wheel of Chance, go to PAGE 8.

If you've already played the Wheel of Chance, go to PAGE 17.

You yank on the reins. But your horse ploughs ahead, pulling you forward—closer and closer to the chopping, chopping, chopping blades. Brad squeezes into the cart and buries his head in his lap.

Patty jumps into the front seat with you. Together you pull on the reins and scream, "Whoa, fellow! Whoa!"

But your horse trots onward. "It's no use," you cry. "We'd better jump!"

You stare over the side. You're riding along a narrow ridge and there's a deep drop that makes your blood run cold! If you jump, you'll plunge to your death!

Then you glance up ahead—and spot a safer place to leap. Great!

You are about to show it to your friends when Brad cries out, "Look at the elves! They chop at set times. If we can get the horse to move faster, we can miss the axes!"

"That's stupid, we should jump!" argues Patty.

What do you think you should do?

If you decide to jump out, go to PAGE 103.
If you urge the horse to gallop, go to PAGE 119.

Carnival workers. The carnival workers who set up the same rinky-dink carnival you go to every summer.

You can't believe your eyes. You must be seeing things!

Patty tries to say something smart, but the only thing she manages is "Huh?"

"Hey, kids!" a worker yells at you. "Get away from that ride. The carnival doesn't start till tomorrow night."

You gaze around in wonder at the faded games, the baby rides, the tacky food stands. For the first time in your life, it all looks great!

"We'll be there!" you shout as you head for your bikes. "This is the greatest carnival I've ever seen!"

THE END

Seconds later your head and the back of your feet slam into the wall. You're hanging upside down—in the middle of a gigantic magnetic wheel!

"Are you ready for The Final Challenge?" Big Al asks.

"Of course not!" you say. "LET ME DOWN!"

"We'll let you down—but not until you face The Final Challenge. One spin will decide your fate. If you win, you go. If you lose, you stay here for ever."

Will that be your fate?

Big Al approaches the wheel.

Brad and Patty are holding on to each other.

Your heart is pounding.

Your hands are sweating.

This is it. One spin.

He gives the wheel—with you on it—a hard turn. Where will it stop? Guess!

On PAGE 44?
On PAGE 74?
On PAGE 124?

"Hey, wait up!" you yell to Brad and Patty as you sprint through the Space Coaster gate.

They both ignore you and charge straight ahead. You follow them into a narrow tunnel that leads to the boarding area.

You gaze down at the floor. Black rubber. It makes you walk with a strange bounce.

Every few feet there is a round porthole window. When you glance out of one, you see astronauts planting flags on the moon. You peer out of another. Now they're seated in their capsule. This is amazing, you think. The figures look real. Totally real.

After a long climb, you and Patty and Brad finally arrive at the loading area.

A sleek bullet-shaped capsule *whooshes* up and stops right beside you. It has three sections. Brad climbs defiantly into the last section. You leap into the front. Patty's left with the middle section.

And suddenly you're trapped!

Go on to PAGE 58.

The crowd is closing in. Your pockets are empty—you have nothing to defend yourself with. So you run!

You spot a crack in the wall, next to the wheel. It's small—too small for an adult to squeeze through—but you can probably make it.

"Follow me!" you yell out to Patty and Brad as you squeeze through the opening. It leads to a backstage area—and then to the flap of another tent.

You can hear the crowd behind you, trying to follow you through the crack.

"Come on! We can slip under this tent," you say. For once, no one argues with you.

The three of you duck in and find yourself surrounded by another crowd. They are all seated in chairs. And they don't move. They just stare at you with glassy eyes.

Turn to PAGE 55.

28

What's the big idea? You're going to embarrass the giant into helping you.

"Hey, you. You know, you're a real wimp," you say to the giant.

He looks at you as if he can't believe what he hears.

Patty and Brad look at you as if you're crazy. Maybe you are.

"You wimp," you continue. "You sit here all day, taking orders from that creep, Big Al. And you live in these horrible conditions. Why? Because you're a wimp and you refuse to fight back. You could bend those bars and escape— but you won't. Because you are a wimp— W-I-M-P—wimp."

The giant stands. You gaze up. He's over fifteen feet tall. He lumbers over to you. He isn't smiling.

Is your plan going to work? Is he going to bend the bars to prove you wrong? Or is he going to bend you?

It's out of your control now.

Look out of the window.

If it's sunny out, turn to PAGE 45.

If it's raining or if it's night-time, turn to PAGE 85.

You stumble down the corridor to your right. As you peer from side to side, you are met with hundreds of images of—you! And you look pretty baffled. And scared.

"Hey, I could use some help," you call out.

Silence.

You pound your fist against the wall.

The wall starts to move.

Just a couple of centimetres—a couple of centimetres closer to you!

You take a step back—but the wall behind you is moving, too.

The walls are moving together. They're closing in on you.

You're going to be crushed!

Squeeze over to PAGE 65.

30

You're falling ... falling ... You can't think of anything else to do, so you start flapping your arms like a bird.

At that moment a huge gust of air shoots up from under you and blows you back on to the bridge.

Breathing hard, you run the rest of the way across the rickety span. When you reach the safety of the other side, you glance back. And gasp! The bridge and the sidestalls beyond it have vanished! Only a black void remains!

"Wow! Awesome special effects!" you cry out loud. But was your fall part of the special effects, too? It didn't feel like it.

You spin around to face the House of Horrors. Up close it appears really, really creepy. Cobwebs drip down from its roof and an eerie yellow light glows inside. Cool! Next to the house you spot a sign that reads BOAT TRIP TO NOWHERE. There are amazing speedboats that you can drive yourself.

Which should you try first?

Want to try the Boat Trip to Nowhere? Go to PAGE 88.

Ready for the House of Horrors? Go to PAGE 66.

You snap your head around to the right—where you hear footsteps coming towards you.

You are facing a short man with wrinkly skin and bloodshot eyes. His bushy, black hair resembles a scouring pad—and from the looks of it, it probably feels like one, too. His evil expression makes you cringe.

But he's nothing compared to the "things" behind him—two seven-foot-tall monsters. One has blue horns and bulging red eyes. The other has scaly skin and an alligator snout that snaps open and closed as he eyes you.

The trio all wear lab coats. And from the eager way they're looking at you, you realize that you are the lab rat.

You struggle to escape from the net. But you're trapped in the webbing. Like a fly in a spider's web.

"Welcome to my humble laboratory," the short man says. "I am Dr Frank N. Stone, the mastermind who created the Carnival of Horrors."

The Carnival of Horrors! You don't like the sound of that!

Go to PAGE 89.

32

Your boat glides through the channel at high speed to Booger Bog. Water sprays up into your face. But soon you have to slow down. Trees have suddenly sprung up all around you. You're completely surrounded now by their towering trunks.

In the dark light, their limbs take on the shape of gnarled arms with blackened, bony fingers at the ends. You stare hard at the tree trunks. Could it be? Are they reaching out for you?

You slowly weave the boat through the twisted trunks and branches. They've grown so thick here that you can barely pilot your boat through them.

The trees rustle as if they're whispering to each other. Their limbs begin to sway. As you glide carefully through the water, the leaves slap against your face. *Slap. Slap. Slap.*

Your heart starts hammering away in your chest. This is really scary. Just how far *is* nowhere? you begin to wonder. Something swipes at your hair! What *was* that?

Turn to PAGE 105.

You glance once more at the dwarf. He lets out an evil cackle. That's it—there's no way you can trust him. Besides, you can hear music up ahead. You're sure you must be near an exit.

"No, thanks. I don't need any help," you mumble.

He shrugs. "Oh, yes, you do," he says. But then he sprints off.

You walk in the direction of the music. But after five minutes, you realize that you're not getting anywhere.

Maybe you should have followed the dwarf. You start to think about Patty and Brad. Are they okay? you wonder.

Just when you think you'll be wandering these tunnels for the rest of your life, the passageway ends! Now you're facing two doors—one red and one blue. Which one should you try? You might as well flip a coin!

Get a coin. Flip it and check whether it comes up heads or tails.

If it comes up heads, take the blue door to PAGE 57.

If it comes up tails, take the red door to PAGE 104.

"Let's go on the rides first!" you say. "That roller coaster looked awesome!"

"Okay," Patty agrees. "Over this way!" she yells as she charges over to it.

When you reach the rides, you can only stare in amazement. These are the most fantastic rides you've ever seen. The towering roller coaster ... the soaring speedboats ... the twisty slides! Every one is in motion. Whizzing, whirling, doing loop-the-loops. And they're all empty! No riders. No people in line!

"Cool!" Patty exclaims. "We have the whole place to ourselves."

Brad's face turns a little green as his gaze swings from the Supersonic Space Coaster to the Doom Slide. "Do you think they have rides that don't go upside down?" he asks.

"Come on! Let's check out the coaster!" Patty calls to you and Brad. Then they run off to its starting gate.

You stop and crane your neck to gaze up at the coaster's first hill. And you gasp!

Quick! Go to PAGE 47.

Five minutes later, the three of you are sneaking down a dark alley. Brad is so frightened, he's practically walking on top of you.

The alley is littered with large cardboard boxes and overflowing rubbish bins. And it smells like dead fish.

"Hey! Quit stepping on my shoe," you say to Brad.

"I'm not stepping on your shoe," he shoots back. "I'm not anywhere near your stupid shoe."

You glance down. And nearly scream.

Brad's right. He's not stepping on you. But about a dozen rats are.

You shake your foot wildly. The rats scurry off.

Brad catches sight of the rats and tries to bolt.

You and Patty quickly pull him back.

"Hey! Look!" Patty says, pointing up ahead. "A door!"

On the door you see a big sign that reads KEEP OUT, so . . . you go in.

Go to PAGE 13.

36

You turn back and head in the other direction. Your reflections bounce off the walls at crazy angles. Are you walking straight, or have you rounded a corner? There's no way to tell. Yet this time you're sure you're going the right way!

"Over here!" a voice calls. "Turn left again!"

Turn left again? Now you are really confused. If you turn left again, will you finally escape?

Turn to PAGE 118.
HELP!

You cover your head with your hands and try to run into a thick grove of trees. But the bat circles in front of you and dives again.

"Stop it! Stop it!" you scream.

As you turn and race towards some low bushes, you remember the stories—the horrible stories about bats making nests in people's hair. And the only way to get them out was to shave your head . . .

Those stories weren't true—were they?

You spot a big stick in the wet dirt and scoop it up.

The bat swoops down at you once more and—*FWAP!* You hit it.

The bat falls to the ground.

And you see it's on a wire.

It's a mechanical bat.

All part of the ride, you think. You think about the boat ride. Boy, they really make things seem real at this carnival, you think. You feel much better when you gaze up ahead. There's a clearing.

But when you see what's there—you scream!

Turn to PAGE 93.

"Got a winner, got a winner," the parrot squawks. "You've won twenty-five points, plus anything you want in the prize room. Step this way."

Eagerly you follow the bird into a storeroom behind the booth. It's packed with the weirdest assortment of junk you've ever seen. Dusty old catalogues, stuffed rats, a collection of axes, and portraits of headless people holding their own heads!

"So pick something. It's getting late," the parrot says.

Not this garbage, you think. Then you spot a shelf of small cans with bright labels: PLAY AND GLOW, CLAY SLIME, and MONSTER BLOOD. Monster Blood? Hey, isn't that the magic stuff you read about in GOOSEBUMPS?

"I'll take the Monster Blood," you decide.

"Excellent choice," the parrot remarks.

As you quickly leave the room with your prize, you wonder, is twenty-five points enough? What do you do next?

If you want to spin again for more points, go to PAGE 9.

If you haven't played Guess Your Weight on Mars yet, go to PAGE 72.

If you have played Guess Your Weight on Mars, go to PAGE 17.

You close your eyes. When you open them, your car lunges forward with a burst of speed—and you loop-the-loop. Your mouth drops open to scream, but no sound comes out.

Now your car starts to plunge downward—like a lift out of control. Your heart pounds in your chest. This is the fastest and best roller coaster you've ever been on! As you near the bottom, you slow down. You begin to catch your breath. And then you see what's up ahead. A huge black hole—a tunnel!

As you shoot towards the open mouth of the tunnel, you begin to scream again. The door of the tunnel is about to close!

Snap! The door comes crashing down—behind your car. You breathe out a long sigh. But now you're in a tunnel so dark that you can't see a thing.

Scary! But not nearly as scary as what happens next.

What happens? Turn to PAGE 94 to find out!

40

"Five, four, three, two, one. We have lift-off," a mechanical voice announces.

To your horror, the rocket blasts off! You're slammed against the side of the capsule with hurricane force. Seconds later, you've left Earth's atmosphere.

A recorded message comes on: "Congratulations. You are the perfect weight for our Mars explorer. We'll be monitoring your trip and will bring you back in approximately twenty years— with a plus or minus ten-year margin of error in case something goes wrong. But do not worry. Nothing can go wrong ... go wrong ... go wrong."

THE END

"What do you mean the magic number could save my life?" you ask Madame Zeno. But the fortune-teller doesn't answer. She stares off into space. She seems to have fallen into a deep trance.

You don't really believe her—these fortune-tellers are all fakes, but you memorize the number anyway. *1–3–2, 1–3–2. I picked red instead of blue*, you chant to help you remember.

Madame Zeno puts the card back in the deck. She closes her eyes and waves you away with her jewelled hand.

You guess the fortune-telling is over, so you leave the tent to search for Patty and Brad.

You squint under the bright lights of the side-stalls, scanning all the game booths. But you can't find them.

You're trying to figure out which way to go when you spot Big Al coming towards you. He's not alone. He's leading a large group of people. As they come closer, you hear that they are chanting something. What is it?

"Play or pay. Play or pay."

What does that mean?

Turn to PAGE 16 to find out.

42

A wave of panic washes over you as the walls crumble around you. You throw your arms over your head and close your eyes.

Then silence. The shaking stops.

When you open your eyes, the room and all the costumed people have vanished. And you are outside—in the rides area! But the biggest surprise of all is that you spot Patty and Brad!

"Boy, am I glad to see you," you say, racing over to them. "Where have you guys been?"

Brad shakes his head. "You wouldn't believe the rides we went on!"

"We've got to get out of here before midnight," you say. Quickly you tell your friends about the warning from the lady with the red parasol.

"No problem," Patty says. "Look. I'm sure the exit is right over there past that ride called the Hall of the Mountain King."

"No, it's that way—near the sign that says HALLOWE'EN EXPRESS," Brad insists.

Which way do you think is the right way?
Hallowe'en Express? Then turn to PAGE 108.
Mountain King? Then turn to PAGE 107.

You are about to scream. It seems like the only sensible thing to do.

And then you remember the sign.

Reptile Petting Zoo.

You have an idea. It's a crazy idea, you know. But everything in this carnival is crazy.

You can feel the alligator's hot breath on your arm. But instead of pulling your arm back, you stretch it out!

"What are you doing?" Patty screams.

Your fingers reach out. Out over the alligator's open snout to the top of his head.

And you pet him.

"Nice alligator," you purr as you stroke his scaly head.

Your arm trembles, but you don't stop. And slowly—very slowly—the creature's mouth begins to shut.

Then he rolls over and falls asleep!

You slip quietly off the log, charge for the shore—and plough right into Big Al!

"Well, well, well. Look who we have here," Big Al sings out. "Come with me. It's time for The Final Challenge."

You have no choice. Follow Big Al to PAGE 84.

44

You're spinning round and round. Everything is a blur. You can't see, but you hear the crowd chanting, "FI-NAL! FI-NAL! FI-NAL!"

And then the wheel stops.

A huge gasp escapes from the audience.

Did you win or lose?

Neither. You stopped on SPIN AGAIN.

Go back to PAGE 25 and spin again.

The giant looms over you. He's as tall as the tree outside your house—and a lot meaner. His huge lips part and he says, "You hurt my feelings."

Then he begins to cry.

"I am not a wimp. I am not," he says between huge sobs.

He certainly looks like a wimp.

Turn to PAGE 98.

You're falling . . . falling . . . everything passes
as if you're dropping in slow motion. Is this . . .

THE END?

Yes.

The tracks stretch up so high that they seem to touch the clouds. Your gaze follows one of the cars speeding around a sharp curve. It looks like the space shuttle. You notice that it has a safety harness that locks over your body—you've seen those before. They keep you in when the ride turns upside down. You didn't want to admit it before, but, like Brad, riding upside down is not your favourite thing.

Still, the coaster does look amazing—one part enters a tunnel—and you can see that the cars go fast. Really fast!

You're just about to walk through the Space Coaster gate when you hear spooky organ music coming from behind you. You turn around. Looming in the distance is a dark and creepy haunted house.

You gaze down at your map. It's called the Little House of Horrors. Hmmm. You love haunted houses. And this one really looks scary.

Now you're not sure what to do. You won't have time for everything. The coaster or the haunted house? Decide now.

If you decide to join Patty and Brad on the Space Coaster, get on board on PAGE 26.

If you want to go to the House of Horrors alone, go to PAGE 64.

48

"Come on!" Patty cries. "Come on!"

Then, without another word, she races off. You and Brad dash after her.

I hope Patty knows what she's doing, you think as you try to catch up. Because right now, it doesn't look that way.

Patty leads you through a maze of underground passageways. Then, just as you're about to yell, "Stop!"—she does. And you find yourself standing outside, in front of a barbed-wire fence!

Up ahead, you spot an opening.

"Let's go in!" Patty says.

The three of you creep through the fence and trudge through some tall, wet grass. You gaze around. It's far too dark to see.

But you can hear perfectly. And the sounds that reach your ears make your skin crawl.

Slithering. You definitely hear slithering.

And hissing.

You want to leave. You spin around, but you can't find the opening in the fence! You do see something else. A sign!

Hurry to PAGE 60.

The wheel stops on FREE SPIN. You are ready to try again. But the stupid parrot flies over and latches on to your shoulder.

"Ouch! That hurts," you cry.

"Free spin, free spin, you're going on a free spin."

"Turn me loose," you command. When you swivel your head to glare at the bird, a scream freezes in your throat. The parrot has ballooned into an enormous vulture. His black, beady eyes pierce right through you. He digs his razor-sharp claws deeper into your shoulder.

Run!—your every survival instinct shouts. But the bird of prey has other ideas. One of them is dinner—with you as the main course.

The big bird snatches you by the back of your shirt as if you were a rag doll. Kicking and screaming and using every defensive move you learned from karate class, you struggle for your life. But it's no use. With a jerk he lifts you off the ground.

And suddenly you have a frightening view of the carnival from ten metres . . . twenty metres . . . thirty metres up.

Fly on to PAGE 50.

50

Thummp, thump, thump. Your heart bangs loudly inside your chest. What kind of carnival is this, you wonder, where a free spin is more like a death sentence?

You circle a green clump of treetops. You're really dizzy now. You want to close your eyes. But you know it's not a good idea—since you're flying thirty metres high without a plane or a parachute.

As you circle closer to the treetops, you are met with a horrifying view. Five baby vultures in a nest, five very hungry babies, with mouths gaping wide open.

The end is near. You are going to wind up as a take-home dinner. Unless you can somehow force the vulture to let you go. Frantically, you reach into your pockets!

If you've won a chocolate bar at one of the Games of Chance, go to PAGE 76.

If you haven't, go to PAGE 115.

You can't take on both monsters, so you decide to wait until one of them leaves the room.

You grab hold of Dr Stone's hand. He's a lot stronger than he looks. With one small tug, he pulls you free of the web.

Then he turns to the monsters. "Okay," he barks. "Adjust the net. It's time to practise spiking.'

Spiking? What does he mean by that?

The monsters leap up. They rub their hands together in evil delight. Then they untie the net and head to the back of the room, where two huge poles rest on the floor.

You close your eyes—and hope that when you open them, you'll see that this was all a dream. A really bad dream.

But when you open your eyes, you know it's not a dream. No—it's a volleyball game. The net has been tied to the poles—and guess what position you play? That's right. You're the ball! Watch out for those two-handed spikes! They can be pretty painful!

THE END

52

Just as the clock strikes twelve, the train enters a tunnel.

You hold your breath, wondering what you'll see when you reach the other end.

Chug. Chug. Chug.

The choo-choo slowly pulls out of the tunnel— and you are surrounded by carnival workers— everywhere!

Chug to PAGE 24.

Oh, no! You think the space lady guessed right! Now what's going to happen?

The two guards shove you into the space chamber.

It's a clear, narrow tube that rises farther up than you can see.

As the door slams shut behind you, one of the guards barks, "Get on the scales!"

You step up on the scales—and it shows just how right the space lady's guess was.

You press the chamber-door release, but it's stuck.

You try again. It doesn't budge.

Maybe it's locked from the outside.

"Hey! I can't get out!" you yell to the guards. But they simply wave.

"Hey, let me out!" Now you're angry. "Let me out!"

All at once the room starts to shake and rattle. *RRRRRRRR*. The thrust of powerful rocket engines echoes in your ears. It sounds as if you're being launched into space. But that's impossible, isn't it?

Go to PAGE 40.

Your Hallowe'en Express car pulls up in front of a cottage and the cottage door opens with a creak. You all jerk your heads up to peer at the door. You see a skeleton wearing an evil smile. And he lunges right for *you*!

"Trick or treat!" he screeches. Then he stretches out his bony hands to snatch you!

You pound on the accelerator, and the car shoots forward—out of the skeleton's grasp!

Your heart begins to race as the car speeds out of control. You tear through an eerie forest, speed past more cottages—but still you don't see a way out.

And then it comes into view—a service exit!

All you have to do is stop the car, jump out, and scramble through the fence, and you'll be free.

You check your watch—five minutes to midnight!

"Oh, no!" Patty screams. "Quick, turn left! Don't stop!"

Turn left! And go to PAGE 83.

They're dummies. That's why they don't move!

"They've got to be here somewhere," you hear Big Al's voice boom outside the tent.

"Hey! This dummy looks just like the one in that GOOSEBUMPS book," Patty says.

"You mean *Night of the Living Dummy?*" Brad asks.

Great! you think. Your friends are chatting about books minutes before you're about to be attacked by a mob. Then you get an idea.

"Remember those magic words that brought the dummy to life in that book?" you ask your friends. "Maybe we can bring this guy to life and he'll help us—he *was* pretty tough."

Your friends agree—it's worth a try.

If you think the words are karru marri odonna loma molonu karrano, go to PAGE 69.

If you think the words are oooopah lupah, dummie dupah, go to PAGE 82.

You leap out of the boat. The putrid brown water splashes into your mouth. Gross!

You swim a few strokes and suddenly find your knees scraping the bottom of the bog. The water here is less than a foot deep. Unbelievable! You were practically inches away from safety the whole time!

Slogging through the brown foam, you wade to shore. Your clothes are dripping wet and smell like a sewer. Well, look on the bright side, you remind yourself. At least you didn't go down with your boat.

But your troubles aren't over yet. You're standing in a dank, eerie forest that surrounds the lake. Creepy screeches echo through the night mist. And you're totally lost.

The wind starts to blow. Shivering, you wrap your arms around your shoulders and wonder where your friends are and what they are doing.

Then—*POW!* Something black and furry swoops down at you! You duck your head, but it comes at you again and again.

A huge bat!

Turn to PAGE 37.

You open the blue door and peer through. You're staring down a long dark passageway. At least you think it's long. It's difficult to tell. It's pitch-black. You don't know what to do.

"Maybe I should have picked the other door," you say to yourself. "I'm getting out of here!"

But the blue door has locked behind you! Now you're sure you made the wrong choice. But there's nowhere to go but forward.

Your knees begin to tremble as you inch your way down the dark hallway.

The passage ends in a bright burst of light. And in front of you, a tall purple mountain rises hundreds of feet into the air.

You breathe out a long sigh of relief. You're out of the dark!

You study the mountain. It looks so real! But cut into its side, you spot a doorway. Above it a brightly painted sign reads: DOOM SLIDE. WILL YOU BE THE ONE TO SLIDE FOR EVER?

Turn to PAGE 135.

58

Steel bars plunge down from above and drop across your lap and chest, pinning you in place. You can't move at all. Even your head is held by super-strong headphones that clamp over your ears. A voice comes through them announcing: "Five, four, three, two, one, BLAST OFF!"

You hear a huge bang. Smoke and fireworks fill the air as your car starts up the first big hill. Your head presses back against the seat as you climb higher and higher. That first hill is endless, but the view is awesome. From the top, you can see the sidestalls, the haunted house, and a shadowy swamp. You can't believe how big the carnival is!

"Neat!" Patty yells. "There's AHHHH—"

Whatever she was going to say turns into a wild scream as the rocket plunges down the other side of the hill. The wind whips at your face. You are pressed back so hard, you feel like a pancake. Everything passes in a fantastic blur.

As your car shoots up to the top of the next hill, you're laughing and screaming at the same time. This is great, you think! But then you make a big mistake.

Turn to PAGE 39.

Blue is your favourite colour. You turn the blue card over.

There is a message: *Help us! You are our only hope. Hurry to the back door of the freak show. Signed, The Freaks.*

"What does this mean?" you ask Madame Zeno. She stares deep into your eyes. Her lips tremble. She leans forward. She's about to speak.

And then the lights go out—and a blood-curdling scream rips through the dark!

You start to bolt for the door when a dim light suddenly flickers. You stare across the table. Madame Zeno is gone!

You reach out to take the card. And it bursts into red-hot flames! In seconds, the entire tent fills with thick smoke. Flames shoot across the floor. You run for the door.

Outside you gulp the fresh air. Whew! You made it.

You glance back. No smoke. No fire. No tent! Everything has disappeared! What should you do now?

If you decide to help the freaks, go to PAGE 11.

If you don't want to help the freaks, go to PAGE 113.

"There's a sign!" you call out to Patty and Brad. "Let's see what it says."

The three of you race through the wet grass. Your socks are drenched. And your trainers squeak as you run. But that's not the sound that's sending chills down your spine.

It's the hissing. It's growing louder.

"I'm not sure I want to read that sign," you call out to Patty and Brad.

"I know what you mean!" Patty shouts back. "I have a feeling we're not going to like what it says."

And you don't. You reach the sign and read it aloud. "Reptile Petting Zoo! Whoever heard of a Reptile Petting Zoo! What kind of carnival is this anyway?"

"This carnival is e-evil," Brad stammers.

You're about to agree when you notice the grass in front of you is swaying. Something is slithering through it. Something big. And then it comes into view.

"Snake!" Brad cries.

You know you have to run—but which way? Left or right?

If you run to the left, turn to PAGE 125.
If you run to the right, turn to PAGE 12.

You're too scared to turn around. And too scared not to. Risking a glance over your shoulder, you see a large, dark shape behind you. It's a big man. No. You squint hard. It's dark and hairy with muddy leaves and green vines trailing from its body. It's some sort of swamp monster!

You run as fast as you can. Your chest is on fire. The swamp monster is gaining on you.

You know you should keep running, but your heart feels as if it's about to explode. You have to stop.

You turn and stare right into the swamp monster's bloody eyes. "Neat costume," you say hopefully.

Good try—but the swamp monster isn't wearing a costume. He's real and this, unfortunately, is really . . .

THE END

62

You decide to wait for Big Al.

"Big Al has to free the freaks," you say to Patty and Brad. "If he doesn't, we'll tell him we're calling the police!"

"Free the freaks?" Big Al says, bursting into the room. "The freaks are free to go any time. This prison is just part of the show. Did you pull that 'free us' joke on him?" Big Al laughs heartily.

"He'ssss lying," the Snake Lady says. "We're prisonersssss."

"Oh, come now," Big Al says. "You're not prisoners." And with that he unlocks all the cell doors. Then he turns to you and your friends.

"As you can see, the freaks are free. Now, come with me. You haven't even tried one game here."

"Don't go with him. It's a trick!" the Snake Lady cries.

Should you go with Big Al?

Who's telling the truth? Big Al or the Snake Lady?

If you want to go with Big Al, turn to PAGE 84.

If you trust the Snake Lady, turn to PAGE 102.

Bump.

A chute opens up. You land head first on soft grass.

You blink several times. A long sigh escapes from your lips. It wasn't the Doom Slide after all.

As you climb to your feet you hear someone call your name.

You glance up and shout for joy. It's Brad! And Patty's there, too!

You tell them about your scary ride on the slide—about how you thought you'd slide forever.

"Cool!" Patty exclaims. "Let's all ride it this time!"

"No!" you tell her. "This carnival is too weird. And dangerous. Something's not right. We have to get out of here. Now!"

"Yeah," Brad agrees. "The faster, the better."

"I have an idea," Patty announces. You and Brad huddle around her. "I spotted a back way out of here. But it's a little risky. We have to squeeze through a barbed-wire fence—and it's guarded by the carnival's security forces. But we should try!"

Are you going to listen to Patty?

Follow Patty? Turn to PAGE 48.

You choose not to take the back way out? Go to PAGE 86.

64

The House of Horrors! You have to see it. You just have to!

"I'll catch up with you guys later," you call to Patty and Brad. "I'm going to check out the haunted house."

You glance down at your map for directions. The rickety wooden bridge over to your left appears to lead straight there.

As you start across the bridge, the wooden planks creak under your feet. Then the bridge begins to sway. You look down. A long way down. The bridge spans a deep, rocky gorge. Gulping, you grab the handrail. You move slowly. A strong wind blows up from the canyon below. The bridge is swaying wildly now, tossing from side to side.

A massive spear of lightning splits the sky. Thunder rumbles so loudly you jump and lose your balance. "Help!" you scream as you tumble right over the side—and plunge towards the jagged rocks below!

How can you save yourself?

Make a grab for the side of the bridge? Turn to PAGE 46.

Flap your arms and try to fly? Turn to PAGE 30.

The walls are closing in faster now.

You throw your arms out and try to push them away. But it's hopeless. You're going to be crushed like an insect.

You suck in a deep breath—it could be the last breath you take.

The floor opens beneath your feet!

You drop down. Down. Down. Down. A long, agonizing scream escapes from your throat as you tumble through space.

Will you ever hit bottom?

"Incoming player," you hear a commanding voice shout. "Stations, everybody."

A layer of webbing catches you like one of those nets trapeze artists use. Gasping, unable to understand what's happening, you bounce up and down.

Bounce to PAGE 31.

66

You start up the brick path to the House of Horrors. Suddenly someone sneaks up behind you and taps you on the shoulder. You spin around and jump back.

Standing in front of you is a bony skeleton.

And it talks.

"Don't go in there," the skeleton says. "Or you'll end up like me . . ."

You stare in terror at the hideous creature. Then you burst out laughing.

"Wow! You guys really want to make the haunted house totally creepy. This is going to be great!" you say.

You're still chuckling as you push open the giant oak door of the House of Horrors. It swings back with a long, loud creak.

You step inside and find yourself in a narrow hallway. The door slams shut behind you and the hall turns darker than a starless night. "I can't even see my hands!" you exclaim.

You stumble ahead slowly, pressing your palms against the walls to guide you.

When will this tunnel end?

Look for a way out on PAGE 80.

Thrumpff! Your foot ploughs into the doctor's stomach again. But this time, it smashes right through it. And hits . . . solid steel!

The crunch of metal echoes in the room—along with the doctor's screams. "Aiiii!" he wails like a siren.

You gaze into the gaping hole made by your trainer. Thousands of circuits and wires burn and crackle inside it. The doctor is a robot! Well, an ex-robot now. Your kick totally destroyed him.

That's the good news.

The bad news is heading towards you. It's the monster with the blue horns and red, bulging eyes.

You scramble out of the net and dash towards the door. But the monster is too quick for you. His tentacle arms shoot out and snatch you. Giant suckers at the ends of his wrists circle your throat.

You gasp for air as the monster pins you against the wall. Can you free yourself from his oozing grasp?

Try, on PAGE 91.

You slowly lower yourself on to the slide. You start to stretch out your legs when the bottom tilts underneath you and throws you forward. You're sliding! Fast!

The surface must be made of some kind of special material because you're zooming down at top speed.

You hold your breath as you fly through the blackness. A bump sends you bouncing into the air. You scream. And scream.

When is it going to end?

Oh, no! Could this be the Doom Slide?

You hear screams echo in the darkness. You twist around. But you don't see anyone.

The ghostly screams grow louder—in front of you, next to you, behind you. Screaming and sliding. And sliding. Never stopping.

You gasp for breath. And then you hear it.

A voice cuts through the blackness. Through the screams. A voice that cries, "Welcome to the rest of your life. Welcome to the Doom Slide!"

THE END

"Karru marri odonna loma molonu karrano."
You say the magic words and—the dummy
comes to life!

He opens his mouth and speaks. "Hey, you.
Your face reminds me of a wart I once had
removed."

"Come on," you plead. "We're the ones who
brought you back to life. Aren't you going to be
nice to us? We need your help."

"I'm sorry," the dummy says. "I'm sorry you're
so ugly . . ." Then he laughs at his own lame
joke.

You stare at him and his face grows serious.
"You brought me to life," he says slowly, "but
now you are my slaves.

"For ever—until . . .

"THE END."

---

*Wait! This isn't the way this is supposed to
end. Quick—you have one last chance. If the fortune-teller told you a secret number, go to that
page now!*

"Nine . . . ten . . ."

"Brad, shut up. Look at this!"

You point to the letters on the front of the train car.

You've been staring at them the whole time. Why didn't you notice them before?

"What about the letters?" Patty says sharply.

"Eleven . . ."

"Don't you see what they say?" you shoot back.

"Right-Way Railroad," Patty reads. "So what?"

The chants of the merry-go-round people echo in your head. *There's only one right way. There's only one right way.*

Could it be?

"Twelve!"

Now what?

Turn to PAGE 52.

Sorry. It's not your lucky day. As you dash towards the sign, the giant crane scoops the three of you up and drops you off into a hollowed-out log. You barely have time to sit up straight before the craft reaches the waterfall!

You hold your breath as the log teeters on the fall's edge. As it plunges over, you scream.

A hard spray smacks you in the face and drenches your clothing as you race down the long slide. At the bottom, the log hits a pool of water and sinks.

You're still holding your breath as you wait to bob to the surface again. But it never happens. You keep going down.

Your last thought is that you're going to set a world record for holding your breath underwater.

You'd better set a world record for closing the book and starting over again. Maybe next time you dive in you'll have better luck.

THE END

You step up to the Guess Your Weight on Mars booth. A woman in a space suit motions you inside a gate. You pass through and find yourself in the middle of a courtyard that looks just like a miniature launching site—complete with its own rocket!

"Security check," the lady says as she presses your hand on to a fake scanner.

"So how does this game work?" you ask.

"I'll guess how much you weigh on Mars," she explains. "Then you'll enter the planet simulation chamber and stand on the scales. If I'm wrong by more than one pound up or down, you win a giant chocolate bar."

"What if you guess right?"

The space lady doesn't say anything at first. She just smiles. A nasty smile. Then she answers.

"You lose," is all she says.

Go to PAGE 18.

Your reflexes are great. You jumped out fast enough and escaped the ghost—*that* ghost. But you didn't see the other one behind the car—waiting for you.

Your heart hammers away in your chest as it circles you. Round and round and round.

"It's all right," you tell yourself over and over. "It's not real. This is just a ride in an amusement park."

You're still telling yourself that as the ghost plucks you off your feet.

His black lips part.

He opens his mouth—wider and wider. Until it's as wide as an entrance to a cave.

Then he stuffs you inside.

Instantly you feel light-headed, then light all over. You peek down at your hands.

You can see straight through them. You've been turned into a ghost! And as your senses fade, you hear a distant bell chime twelve times. Too bad. The Carnival of Horrors will be one of your favourite haunts—for ever!

THE END

Round and round you go. The world is a blur of colours. You can hear the crowd screaming. "FI-NAL! FI-NAL!"

And the wheel stops.

"Ahhhhhh," the crowd gasps.

What does it mean?

"YOU WIN," Big Al says. "Now come this way to collect your prize and go home."

Turn to PAGE 131.

The three of you duck inside the Hall of the Mountain King!

A painted backdrop of rounded snowcapped mountains rises on your left. Up in the mountains a big stone castle rests in the sunshine. A group of cheerful elves pick flowers in the castle's garden.

To your right, you spot the ride—wooden carts pulled by real horses. "Come on!" you call to your friends. "Jump in a cart. This is great. We'll be out of here in no time." No time—that reminds you. You glance at your watch. 11:45!

You all scramble into one of the carts and grab the reins. Your horse plods forward, and you pass through a painted stone archway.

You gasp. Everything in the painted backdrop is now in front of you. And it has suddenly become real. But different!

The snowcapped mountains rise to black, jagged peaks that pierce the sky. The big stone castle huddles on a scary, dark hill. And the elves—they aren't picking flowers.

They're . . .

Turn to PAGE 96.

76

You dig deep into the side pocket of your jeans—and find it! The chocolate bar you won.

It's a good thing you didn't eat it all—but will the vulture go for it?

Without warning, the big bird starts his final approach, diving straight for the nest. You pull out the chocolate and wave it frantically in front of him. "Treat! Treat!" you holler. These words make your dog at home go wild. But will it work on the vulture?

Yes! He cracks open his beak—just enough for you to wiggle loose. Then you're falling, falling.

You've landed on a giant trampoline.

Fwanggg!

Now you're going up again. Higher this time. Now you're falling again.

Fwanggg—you've bounced up even higher this time.

Every life has its ups and downs, but it looks as if you'll be bouncing up and down for ever—and boy, is it fun!

THE END!
THE END!
THE END!
THE END!

"Let's head for the sidestalls and play some games!" you say.

You, Patty and Brad jog down a wide avenue. Tents of every colour line the street. Carnival music blares from loudspeakers.

You spot a green neon sign flashing above a yellow-striped tent. The sign reads: MADAME ZENO—FORTUNE-TELLER.

"Excellent!" you exclaim. "I'm going in!"

You tell your friends you'll catch up with them in a minute.

You lift the tent flap. Inside, one small candle flickers in the dark. You hear a low voice call out, "Enter my chamber."

There is Madame Zeno, sitting in the shadows. She wears a long red dress dotted with brightly coloured gems. They shimmer in the candlelight. Her black hair tumbles to her shoulders as she bends over a large crystal ball.

"Welcome," she whispers. Then she reaches out and gently lifts your hand. "Let me tell you your future."

To find your future, go to PAGE 78.

78

Madame Zeno studies your hand closely. She traces the lines in your hand with her soft fingers.

"I see horror in your future. In your *immediate* future," she warns.

"Wh-what kind of horror?" you stammer. "What do you mean?"

Madame Zeno releases your hand. She picks up a strange deck of cards. She spreads them out on the table. You notice the cards have pictures—a headless man, a bloody sword, a large, evil eye.

She gathers up all the cards and flips the deck over. Then she deals out a red card and a blue card.

"Turn one over," she commands. "Learn your fate."

Pick red? Go to PAGE 14.
Pick blue? Go to PAGE 59.

The doctor leans over. He's so close now, his sour breath fills your nostrils. Then his fingertips brush your hand and—*POW!* Your foot flies into his stomach! A direct hit!

But nothing happens.

He doesn't scream. He doesn't even moan. In fact, he doesn't seem to notice at all.

He simply smiles at you.

Now you're scared. Really scared. But you know you have to do whatever it takes to get out of there. You have to find your friends and escape from this Carnival of Horrors.

You gather up every ounce of courage and strength you have—and kick him once more. Harder!

And this time something does happen—BIG TIME!

Turn to PAGE 67 to find out what.

80

You turn a corner and are instantly blinded by glaring lights.

You are standing in a room of mirrors. Walls. Floor. Ceiling. All mirrors!

Everywhere you gaze, you are met with reflections of yourself! You take a few steps forward and—*CRACK!* You hit your head on solid glass.

You move one step to the left, and a dozen copies of you move in that direction.

Totally dizzy, you close your eyes. Maybe you can find the exit with your hands. Keeping your eyes shut, you walk until your palms hit against another glass wall. Then you hear a voice. "Come this way. Over here," it calls.

You walk towards the voice—*CRACK*—a solid wall again.

Finally your hands find an open doorway! It leads to a mirrored hallway that goes left and right. Which way will you go?

If you decide to turn right, go to PAGE 29.
If you decide to turn left, go to PAGE 118.

"You're lying!" you yell. "You *are* a robot."

You quickly reach up with both hands and tug at his head. His sharp jaws slash at you. But you're fast. You hold on firmly and pull!

Oh, no! He really is a monster. And he's not happy.

You know you're dead meat, but you have to try one more time. Just to make sure. You give his head one more tug. He laughs. Then he gives *your* head a tug.

Sorry. You were doing so well. But now you've gone and lost your head. The only way you'll be able to face the challenge of the Carnival of Horrors now is to close the book and begin another day. At least then—you'll have a head start.

THE END

"Oooopah lupah dummie dupah." You say the magic words and wait for the dummy to spring to life.

And you wait.

And you wait.

The dummy remains the same.

But something strange is happening to you. What are those feathers sprouting out of your skin? And what's happening to your feet? Are those claws you see growing out of them?

Is it possible that the magic words are turning you—*CLUCK*—into a—*CLUCK*—chicken?

That's eggs-actly what's happening.

Well, you laid an egg this time. Let's hope you won't be too chicken to open this book again and try once more to escape from the Carnival of Horrors.

THE END

You squint hard at the road ahead of you—
and see why Patty wants you to turn. There
they are—the people in the old-fashioned
clothes. Only they don't look the same.

Some have green flesh. Some are deathly
white. Their rotting skin hangs from their
bones.

And they're all reaching out. Reaching out for
you!

"Turn! Turn!" Patty yells.

You spin the wheel sharply to the left to avoid
them. But you can't dodge the ghostly creature
that's rising above you. He's ten feet tall—with
arms so long that they scrape the ground. His
mouth gapes open to reveal hundreds of blackened, rotting teeth.

He swoops down at you. You turn the steering
wheel hard to the right. Too hard—it comes off
in your hands!

"Jump!" you cry. "Jump and run! Run!"

The three of you leap out of the moving car.
But are you fast enough? That depends on how
good your reflexes are.

Try this test and find out. Throw a ball in the
air. Try to clap three times before you catch it.

If you can do it—turn to PAGE 73.
If you couldn't—turn to PAGE 127.

84

Big Al shoves you and your friends into a huge red tent. It seems to be set up for some kind of show. Red carpeted steps lead up to a platform, which sits under a golden arch. The arch twinkles with a thousand coloured lights that spell out: FINAL CHALLENGE.

Trumpets blast as people flood into the viewing area. As they march in, they clap their hands and yell, "FI-NAL. FI-NAL."

Big Al leads you up the carpeted steps. You are standing on the platform now—in front of a shimmering curtain that hangs down from the arch.

The crowd begins to chant, "SUD-DEN DEATH. SUD-DEN DEATH."

"What do you think *that* means?" Patty asks.

You're going to find out on PAGE 123.

The giant hangs over you, flexing his muscles. He squints at you as if you are an insect—ready to be squashed.

"Did you call me a wimp?" he thunders.

You are much too scared to answer.

The giant answers for you. "You're right. I am a wimp!"

And with that, he bends the bars, and you, Patty, and Brad scramble through.

"Follow me," the giant says. "I know a way out of here."

"What about the others?" you ask, pointing to the freaks in the cells that line the wall.

"No problem!" Patty yells, grabbing the keys from a hook on the wall. "Here—catch!"

You quickly unlock all the doors—setting the freaks free!

Turn to PAGE 126.

"I don't know," you say. "I don't think we should take any more risks. Especially not in this crazy carnival."

"Don't you trust me?" Patty demands. Her eyes flash angrily.

You glance at Brad. He stares at the ground.

"I just have a bad feeling about this, Patty. Okay?"

But Patty doesn't answer. She throws her shoulders back and stands up taller. And taller. And taller.

You gasp! Patty is growing! She's nearly ten feet tall!

She reaches out a long arm and grabs you by the wrist. Her nails dig deep into your skin.

You can't move.

You scream as Patty continues to change. Her skin turns green and lumpy. Horns sprout from her head. And her teeth grow into sharp fangs.

You remember the horrible monsters on the walls of the slide. Patty has turned into one of them!

"Let me go. Please!" you plead.

"Too bad you didn't trust me," she growls. "I can't have you ruining my plans." Her nails sink deeper into your flesh.

"Ha-ha-ha!" she cackles. Then she wraps her slimy mouth around your arm and bites down. Hard!

THE END

You're staring at a sign that reads: WORLD'S FREAKIEST FREAK SHOW! The three of you gape at the pictures.

There's the Three-headed Man with the ugliest collection of faces you've ever seen. And the Snake Lady—a young blonde girl with a beautiful face and the body of a slithering snake.

"This is, uh—uh—" you start to say. But you don't finish. Because a large hand has come down on your shoulder. Hard.

You slowly turn and gaze up at a huge man with shoulders wider than a refrigerator. He has coal-black eyes with a thick moustache to match. He looks strong enough—and mean enough— to throw you over the fence with one hand.

"What are you doing?" his deep voice booms. "You're not allowed in here," he says, pointing directly at *you*.

"We're sorry," you say, hoping you appear sorry and not just scared. "We wanted to look around. That's all. But we'll leave. Right now."

His eyes stare into yours. He clamps both hands down on your shoulders and says, "You're not going anywhere!"

Uh-oh. Quick! Better turn to PAGE 4.

You head towards the Boat Trip to Nowhere. At the dock, you spot a stubby guy with long arms slouching against one of the mooring posts. In the strange light of the swamp, his skin shines with an oily, green glow. And his ears and nose are as craggy as tree bark.

"Step right up," he calls in a gravelly voice.

He pulls one of the motorboats over. It's red with a silver racing stripe! "You can do fifteen knots in these babies," he says. "But stay away from the tree stumps."

You watch the little man's sharp green fingernails tearing the mooring rope apart. As soon as the boat is free, you jump in, step on the accelerator, and roar away from the dock.

The wind blows hard against your face. You're flying over the water. This is totally cool! You head for a channel that you see up ahead. Too bad you didn't notice that sign that reads: TO BOOGER BOG.

Enter the bog on PAGE 32.

Dr Stone extends a long bony hand to pull you from the net. When you peer into his face, his eyes roll up into his head.

"Pleased to meet you," he rumbles.

Did he say, "Pleased to meet you" or "Pleased to eat you"? You're not sure, and you don't want to hang around to find out.

I've got to get out of here, you think.

As the doctor lowers his hand a bit more, you wriggle your right foot free of the netting. If you give him one hard kick in the stomach, maybe you can make a run for the door.

But what about the monsters? Can you dodge them?

You change your mind. "I'll wait—play it cool until at least one of the beasts leaves the room," you say to yourself.

Then you change your mind again. "No. I'd better make my escape now!"

The doctor looms centimetres away. And you're still not sure what to do. You'd better decide fast!

Try to kick the doctor and run? Turn to PAGE 79.

Wait until one of the monsters leaves and the odds are better than three against one? Turn to PAGE 51.

NO!

At the last minute, you wrench the steering wheel hard to the left. The side of your boat clears the tree with a sickening scrape.

You breathe a sigh of relief, but it ends in a groan. A huge, sharp root below the water has just ripped into the bottom of your boat. You hear a tearing sound, then gurgling as the cockpit starts to fill with water.

"Now what?" you mutter.

Then through the mist you spot another boat. But it's some distance away.

"Hey, over here!" you cry out.

Did they hear you? You cry out again. Then you glance behind you. More than half your boat is underwater—and you're going down fast.

What should you do? Keep yelling for help? Or try to swim for safety? Make your choice— QUICK!

If you decide to wait to be rescued, go to PAGE 100.

If you decide to swim for it, go to PAGE 56.

The red-eyed beast leans against you now, pressing you hard against the wall. The monster moves his face close to yours. The jagged horns at the top of his head nick your cheeks.

You can't bear it any more. You bring your hand up with all your might and shove his head away from yours.

As you watch in horror, the monster's head rolls off its neck. The head tumbles to the floor and lands at your feet.

The eyes glance up at you, and you notice his hideous lips moving. "That hurt," the head says. "That really h-h- . . ."

He never finishes. You've destroyed another robot!

"Almost out of here," you whisper to yourself. Now all you have to do is slip by the crusty, alligator-snout creature guarding the door.

"You robots aren't so tough," you say to him with fake bravery.

"Oh, really?" the scaly beast croaks. "Well, maybe not. But what makes you think that *I* am a robot?"

Turn to PAGE 122.

92

You decide to wait. Someone should be here soon, you think. But after waiting in the space shuttle for at least fifteen minutes, you're not so sure. No one has shown up to rescue you.

A chill runs down your back. You feel as if a thousand pairs of eyes are watching you from the shadows.

Now that you're accustomed to the darkness, you can see dozens of tracks leading in and out of the tunnel.

And then you hear a rustling sound. You freeze. You listen hard. Could it be rats—or something worse?

You draw up your knees and wrap your arms around them tightly. Then you hear a hissing sound—and you smell something odd. It's quite a sweet smell—like heavy perfume. You hold your nose because the smell is making you feel strange. Dizzy. Sick.

Hold your breath and turn to PAGE 20.

What a sight!
You can hardly believe your eyes!
You scream again.
It's Patty and Brad!
"Hey guys, wait up!" you yell.

Quick! Hurry to PAGE 26 and you can go on the Space Coaster with them.

The ride stops.

Dead.

You are sitting in the dark.

Nothing is moving.

"Patty! Brad!" you call.

Silence.

Why don't they answer? They have to be there.

You try to twist around. But you're locked in your harness and clamped in your headrest.

Blinking in the dim light, your eyes dart to the left. Then to the right. You spot dozens of empty space rockets lining the walls. They seem to come in sections—to make longer and shorter space rockets.

Your mind starts working feverishly. Did your section detach from Patty and Brad's section?

Suddenly the silence is shattered. Your seat lock grinds open, and you are released from your harness. You quickly spin around. Patty's and Brad's cars have disappeared! If this is all part of the ride, maybe you should hop out. But if the ride is broken, maybe you should wait for help.

Wait for help to come? Turn to PAGE 92.
Hop out of the car? Go to PAGE 111.

You sit down on the slide and push off. The world tilts as you plunge down. Down, down, down.

You're scared. But you can't help feeling that this is quite cool! Sliding and swirling in the darkness.

Until you hear the screams. The eerie screams that follow you as you twist and turn.

Your heart starts pounding wildly. Oh, no! You must have picked the Doom Slide. You're going to slide for ever!

And, then, *bump*.

A chute opens up. You hit the ground hard. You tumble over and over and finally stop.

You lie on the ground. Panting.

You're outside!

You scramble to your feet and gaze around.

You hear laughter. It seems to be coming from the bright pink building a few feet in front of you.

You walk over to its big pink door and press your ear against it.

Yes. The laughter is definitely coming from inside.

To find out what's so funny, turn to PAGE 117.

. . . they're swinging axes.

Your heart leaps into your throat. The elves move to the roadside now—and they're chopping down the horse-drawn carts ahead of you! One cart splinters into a million pieces before your horrified eyes.

The elves continue on to the next cart. Their sharp blades slice right through it!

Your horse keeps trotting up the steep path. You're heading right for the wildly chopping elves!

"Do something!" Patty cries.

Turn to PAGE 23.

Your hand clamps around the can of Monster Blood in your pocket. Quickly you snap off the lid and the green gunk pours out.

"Look! It's alive!" Brad shouts.

He's right. The Monster Blood oozes from the can, quivers, and appears to stretch and pull itself up! Then it starts to roll and bounce, making horrible sucking sounds.

Great! It's rolling into the crowd, sucking up everything in its path!

"Run!" Big Al screams as the huge green ball rolls over the people in the crowd—sucking them up with a loud plop.

Then the Monster Blood hits the side of the tent. It changes direction.

It's coming after you!

Hurry to PAGE 129.

Well, looks can fool you. He is not a wimp.
And he's very angry—at you.

In the next moment, he scoops you up and hurls you at the cell wall. His throw is so forceful, you smash right through the wall and soar out of the carnival grounds.

Congratulations! You escaped the Carnival of Horrors—but not in one piece.

THE END

"Okay, get me out of here," you say to the dwarf. "Did you help my friends, too?"

The dwarf does not answer. He sprints off and you have to race to keep up with him. Through a confusing maze of twisting tunnels. You're very glad you have a guide.

The dwarf suddenly stops. "That way," he says gruffly, pointing straight ahead.

Before you can blink, he vanishes in a puff of smoke! And you're left standing in front of two doors. One red. One blue. The red one has a sign that reads: DANGER. The blue one has a sign that reads: BIG DANGER.

If you leave by the red door, go to PAGE 104.
If you try the blue door, go to PAGE 57.

"Help! Help! Over here!" you scream, waving your arms wildly in the air.

"Hold on!" a deep voice answers through the heavy mist.

The boat turns and speeds towards you. As it nears, the voice calls out again. "Jump! Jump over!"

Jump? Is he crazy? Can you really jump on to a moving boat?

The boat is coming closer now. Closer. Closer. You stand up. You bend your knees. You're about to jump—and the boat speeds right past you.

But wait! It is circling back now in a nice, slow approach. It glides up to you, and gigantic hands pull you on to the boat.

"You saved me!" you cry.

You gaze up and gasp in surprise. The man in the other boat isn't a man—it's a monster with a drooling snout and rows of jagged teeth.

"Save you? Save you?" the monster repeats.

His red eyes light up. "Save you . . . good idea," he says. "I won't eat you now. I'll save you for a midnight snack!"

THE END (*Burp!*)

You make it! You make it out of the park!

You also make it out of the state!

In fact, the last time anyone saw you, Patty and Brad, you were all a tiny blip on NASA's radar screen.

Congratulations! You escaped from the Carnival of Horrors.

Happy landings!

THE END

102

"I'm not going anywhere with you, Big Al. I believe the Snake Lady!"

"So do I," says Patty.

"Me, too!" Brad echoes.

"That's too bad," Big Al says. Then he turns to the Snake Lady.

"And as for you, Miss Reptilia—I told you, you've been overacting. If these kids believe you, we won't be able to torture them with our real horrors."

"Sorry, boss," she says. "So what do you want me to do with them?"

You can hardly believe it! Real horrors?

"What kind of carnival is this?" you shout.

"The Carnival of Horrorsssssss," the Snake Lady answers—and that's the good news.

Turn to PAGE 120 for the bad news.

"We've got to jump," you tell Patty and Brad. "It's our only chance."

"Okay," Brad agrees as your cart inches up to the chopping elves.

"Come on," you cry. "Now!" But Brad is too paralysed with fear to move. You and Patty grab him and haul him towards the side of the cart.

Your cart has reached the elves! One of them smirks as he lifts his axe.

It's right above your neck.

You picture your head tumbling down the side of the mountain.

With a loud cry, all three of you jump. You land with a thud on a rocky ledge. It breaks your fall. But the rock is too weak to hold all of you.

You scream again as the edge tears loose and the world drops from under your feet. You tumble over and over, down the side of the mountain.

Go to PAGE 109.

104

You push open the red door. Another tunnel lies beyond it. You follow its twists and turns, and you realize that you're sloshing through cold muddy water. It grows deeper and chillier as you go.

With a cold shudder, you decide to head back—until you hear a slurping noise behind you. Whirling around, you watch in horrible fascination as giant earthworms crawl out of the mud. Gross!

There's no way you're going back there. You clench your teeth and slog onward. Up ahead, you see a dim green light. Great! An exit.

As you reach the end of the tunnel, you hear a low growl behind you. At first you try to pretend it's your imagination. But there's no mistaking the sound of thudding footsteps. Getting closer. And closer. And now it's breathing down your neck!

Go to PAGE 61.

It's a tree branch! Grabbing at you. Tugging, tugging at your hair. You can't break free. Its gnarly stubs dig in deeper as you struggle.

Suddenly you feel something wrap itself around your arms. Then your legs. Closing in tighter. Tighter.

You gaze down and see them—black knobby tree limbs twisting around you. Strangling you.

You drop hold of the steering wheel and begin to claw at the branches, ripping them away.

And then you peer up—and see a terrifying sight. It's a huge tree. And you're heading straight for it! You grasp the steering wheel to regain control of the boat. The tree is just inches away.

Are you going to CRASH?!

Turn to PAGE 90.

106

"Unless what?" you scream. "Tell me!"

"You can escape the Carnival of Horrors if you leave before closing time."

"When is closing time?" you shoot back.

"When the last ride stops . . ." the lady whispers. "*At midnight.*"

You glance at your watch—11:40. Twenty minutes—that's not so bad. But how do you get out of here?

As if the lady can read your mind, she says, "There's only one right way."

Then all around you, the crowd begins to chant.

"*Only one right way, only one right way.*" They repeat it over and over again.

"What is it?" you scream. "Which way?"

It's useless. They're not going to tell you.

But it's not midnight yet. There's still time to figure it out.

Until the floor begins to tremble. And the walls begin to shake.

Earthquake!

Turn to PAGE 42.

"Sorry, Brad. I think Patty's right," you tell him as you turn towards the Hall of the Mountain King. "I think I spotted an exit there when we first came in."

Patty runs ahead. "Look!" she cries out. "There's the path. It leads past the Hall of the Mountain King to the exit."

"Yeah, but who are those people up there?" Brad asks. "They're blocking the way."

You peer up ahead and see them—the people in the old-fashioned clothes. And they're still chanting—"*Only one right way, only one right way.*"

"They're not going to let us out!" Brad panics.

"Okay. Okay. I have an idea," you say calmly. "Let's go into the Mountain King ride—maybe we can jump off at the end and sneak past them."

Do you have another choice? No.

If you want to go on the Mountain King ride, turn to PAGE 75.

If you want to go on the Mountain King ride, turn to PAGE 75.

108

"We've got to get out of here, it's almost mid-night," you say as you run towards the Hallowe'en Express ride.

"Hey, maybe we should try one of these cars," Brad says, pointing to the red and orange cars that run on a track.

The three of you crowd into a little car that's really meant for two. You jam your foot on the accelerator, and you're flying!

"All right!" Brad cheers. "We're on our way home! Hey, I wonder why they call this *Hallowe'en* Express?" he asks.

You turn the wheel sharply to the left, and then you know why . . .

Speed over to PAGE 54.

You squeeze your eyes shut and wait for the crash. Finally, you land. You glance up. You're at the foot of the Log Flume ride.

You, Patty and Brad have lots of cuts and bruises, but you're okay! Terrific! you think—until you spot the army of elves with their axes. They're rushing down the mountain towards you! The only escape is to enter the flume ride, so you dash inside.

The Log Flume reminds you of a western logging camp, complete with log cabins, trees, trucks, and a sparkling blue lake.

In the distance, you can hear the buzz of chain-saws. And down by the lake, giant cranes pick up logs and plop them in the water. Some of the logs are hollowed out in the middle with seats for passengers. As you watch, the current catches one. It glides to the edge of a waterfall, plunges over, and shoots down.

As you glance around, you spot an EXIT sign.

Then to your horror, you see a giant crane swinging your way. "Duck!" you scream.

Will you make it to the exit? Is this your lucky day?

If you are reading this book on a Monday, Wednesday, Friday, or Saturday, go to PAGE 114.

If it's a Tuesday, Thursday, or Sunday, go to PAGE 71.

110

Something tells you that this monster is not a robot. This one is for real. Maybe it's the way he stares into your eyes. Or maybe it's the rows and rows of razor-sharp teeth jutting from his mouth.

You take a step back. He takes a step closer. A drop of his drool drips on your hand. It sizzles and burns.

This *is* the end, you figure. You'll never escape the Carnival of Horrors. Never see your family or Patty and Brad again.

The monster lifts his gigantic, clawed hand. He waves it over your head. And you wait for the searing pain as it plunges down to strike you.

But that's not what happens.

The monster slowly lowers his hand and clutches at his own neck, and then—pulls his own head off! And when you discover what's underneath, you know you're still in big trouble!

Quick—head over to PAGE 133.

Your pulse pounds in your ears as you carefully lift yourself out of the car. The tunnel is dark and musty and really creepy. Anything could be lurking in the shadows.

This must be part of the ride, you reason. And the more you think about it, the more convinced you are. You're scared. But you have to admit, this is pretty cool.

In the distance, you spot several red lights that seem to lead to other dimly lit tunnels. You cautiously head towards one of them. Overhead something dark and slimy drips. Splattering on the top of your head. Stinging your forehead.

As you desperately try to wipe the burning slime away, something grabs you by the knees!

Aaaah! You look down. A pair of red-rimmed eyes meet yours. It's a dwarf with scraggy red hair and a toothless smile.

"Want me to lead you out of here, kid?" he asks. You're about to follow the dwarf, but then you stop. Is he part of the ride? He looks really evil. What do you do?

Follow the dwarf? Go to PAGE 99.
Decide not to follow the dwarf? Go to PAGE 33.

112

Yeoow! Someone splashes cold water in your face. Your eyes open.

"Come on! Wake up! It's almost show time," a raspy voice says.

"Show time?" you say, gazing into the eyes of a dwarf. "What show?"

"The Freak Show. You are the Amazing Siamese Triplets."

You glance around and see Patty on one side of you and Brad on the other. You try to pull away from them, but you can't.

"We're stuck together with some kind of glue," Patty says.

"It isn't glue," Brad argues.

"Is too!"

"Is not!"

Well, whatever it is—you are stuck. Stuck between your arguing friends for a long, long time—for ever. And here's something you can't argue about. This really is . . .

THE END

Help some freaks? That's a good one! You laugh.

You think about Madame Zeno, the fire, and the disappearing tent. Totally cool! You wonder who thought up such awesome special effects.

You can't wait to tell Brad and Patty all about it.

You search for your friends in the big wooden booths. Instead you find incredible games of chance. Some test your eye-hand coordination. Others require pure luck. But they all offer the most amazing prizes you've ever seen—CD players, video games, fifteen-speed mountain bikes. You can't wait to play!

You spot a booth with a crowd gathered in front. That's odd, you think. Didn't Big Al say we were the only people at the carnival tonight? You wonder if your friends are in the crowd. You move closer.

"Oh. I get it," you say aloud. "These people must work at the carnival."

You're about to call out to them. Until you see their eyes. Strange, haunted eyes.

See what happens on PAGE 16.

114

This *is* your lucky day.

You duck as the crane swings over your head. "Run!" you shout to your friends.

You glance at your watch—11:55. If you're really lucky, you can still make it out of the carnival by midnight.

You can see the exit up ahead. As you charge through the gate, you feel really hopeful—until you run into Big Al.

He blocks the exit with his huge body. His massive hands are planted on his hips. "No one escapes from the Carnival of Horrors!" he roars.

You've got to find a way out. Now!

To your right is the entrance to Hallowe'en Express—you could try that.

Or maybe you should run down a different path. There's got to be more exits around here somewhere.

Choose fast!

Run down a different path? Go to PAGE 5.
Hallowe'en Express? Go to PAGE 108.

There's nothing in your pocket but lint.

"Help! Save me!" you cry.

The vulture swoops down and drops you in the nest.

The baby vultures approach.

Mouths open—ready to peck you to death . . .

But—good news! They don't eat you. You fall out of the nest instead.

Please, close the book fast, or the next sound you hear will be your body, hitting the ground with an awesome *thud*.

THUD!

Not fast enough. Okay, don't go to pieces. Pull yourself together and prepare to visit the Carnival of Horrors again—the next time you're brave enough to open this book!

THE END

116

ZAP!

Big Al throws a switch and the magnet shuts off. You come flying down to earth—right where Brad and Patty are waiting.

"I've played your stupid game. Now let us go!" you tell Big Al.

Big Al doesn't answer. But the crowd does. "SUD-DEN DEATH! SUD-DEN DEATH! SUD-DEN DEATH!"

The crowd surges towards you. They are not friendly. They back you up against a wall. You're trapped.

Trapped by a mob!

You reach into your pocket, hoping to find something that might help you. Something to save you . . .

If you've won a can of Monster Blood, go to PAGE 97.

If you don't have the Monster Blood, run to PAGE 27.

You open the door and enter a room bursting with people who seem to be waiting for you. You think that's weird until you study them—and realize something even stranger. They're all dressed up in old-fashioned costumes.

"Welcome to the Carnival of Horrors," a tall woman with a red parasol says, smiling. "Nice of you to join us."

The Carnival of Horrors. The words send shivers down your spine.

The woman with the parasol whispers in your ear, "Don't you want to know the secret of the Carnival of Horrors?"

You nod "yes".

"The Carnival of Horrors comes alive in a different place and a different time each night. Tonight we're in your town. Tomorrow we could be in another country! But every place we stop, we *invite* kids like you to join us . . ."

"Thanks for the invitation," you say, "but I gotta go."

"I'm sorry." The lady chuckles. "You can never escape from the Carnival of Horrors," she says solemnly. "Unless . . ."

Unless what? Turn to PAGE 106.

118

You turn left. Somewhere ahead of you, you hear laughter.

"Is somebody there?" you call out.

Silence.

You stare at your reflections in the mirrored hall.

Am I trapped? you wonder. Am I in real danger? Or is this all a big, scary joke? Your heart begins to race.

You inch forward a few more steps—moving towards the laughter. Slowly.

"Over here," a voice calls again. But now the voice seems to be coming from behind you!

Turn to PAGE 36.
HELP!

You take charge of the reins to urge the horse on.

"Giddyup, boy," you and Patty shout. But your horse won't move any faster.

You shoot a glance up ahead. The elves are chopping . . . and a shiny blade . . . is now . . . right over . . . your head!

"No," you scream. "NO! Let me out of here."

You feel a sharp pain. And you realize you've just had the shortest haircut of your life. Unfortunately, they took a little too much off the top.

THE END

120

The bad news is the Snake Lady fooled you.

"Throw them into the large cell with Harold and all the other *prisoners*," Big Al commands.

You are shoved into a dark cell. You hear a *click*. You're locked in. As the Snake Lady leaves with Big Al, you can hear their laughter echo down the hall.

You glance into the other cells and think, the freaks *are* prisoners. They *do* need our help. Then you peer into the darkness of your cell— to find out who Harold is.

There's no way you could miss him. Harold is a giant. He's huge—twice as big as an American football player. His hands are, in fact, the size of two footballs. His arms look like tree trunks.

At first you are afraid of him, but then you think, Hey! He's trapped, too. Maybe we can convince him to help us. And then you get a big idea!

Turn to PAGE 28.

You grab the sides of the slide and lower yourself down. The second you sit, the slide's floor tilts up beneath you and propels you forward.

You shriek!

You raise your arms and scream louder. You slide faster and faster. In total darkness. Darkness so black, you can't even see your own feet in front of you.

Your eyes dart frantically from side to side. Faces suddenly appear in the darkness in bright flashes of light. Faces of hideous monsters with deformed heads and oozing flesh.

But you're moving too fast to focus on them. You slide and slide—until the faces stop flashing and you're covered in the thick, heavy blackness again.

You scream as you round a sharp curve. Your head is spinning. You pick up speed.

When will it end?

Then you hear the screams. Chilling screams that echo through the darkness.

Oh, no! You must have picked the Doom Slide!

Zoom to PAGE 63.

122

The creature slides one step towards you, and with a burning stare says, "I am not a robot. I am not going to shut down. So don't bother with any of your silly, human tricks!"

You stare at him. You study him hard. Is he lying? Is he a robot like the other two? Or could he be a lot more dangerous?

Your knees begin to tremble when you think about never going home—never seeing your family and friends ever again. Tears start to sting your eyes. Angry tears! No carnival—not even a Carnival of Horrors—is going to defeat you!

You stare deeply into the evil eyes of the creature hovering before you.

Robot? Real monster? You finally decide!

If you think the creature is a robot, try to knock his head off on PAGE 81.

If you think he's a real monster or something worse, stay cool on PAGE 110.

"The Final Challenge," Big Al announces. And the crowd goes wild.

Then he turns to you and says, "Remember—the fun games are over. Now you are playing for your life."

"You go first," Big Al says to you. You see Brad and Patty taken off to the side by a huge man in a black hood.

Two red-haired dwarfs in clown costumes scurry up the steps. To your surprise, they fit you with new high-top trainers—trainers with metal studs running up the backs. This is going to be some kind of race, you think. But then you change your mind—when they snap a heavy, metal helmet on your head.

The crowd's cheers grow louder. Big Al throws a switch. The curtain behind you parts and—*Whammo!* The wall behind the curtain turns into a super magnet. You go zinging to the wall like a dart to a bull's-eye.

Zing back to PAGE 25.

124

"FI-NAL! FI-NAL! FI-NAL!" you hear the crowd yelling as you spin round and round.

You're getting dizzy. Really dizzy. So dizzy that you faint.

Your eyes flutter open on PAGE 112.

"This way!" You wave to Patty and Brad.

The three of you turn to the left and keep running—straight into a pond!

"Why didn't you tell us to stop?" Patty whines.

"Don't complain to me!" you shout back. "We followed *you* through the fence!"

You turn around and slog your way back to shore. Patty and Brad make it there first. You are a few feet away—when you see *it*.

An alligator.

With its mouth gaping open—revealing two rows of razor-sharp teeth.

You freeze.

Patty spots the alligator and yells, "Quick! There's a log! Jump on it!"

You scramble up on the log, but it's no use. You're still an easy target.

The alligator opens its huge mouth even wider. He slithers right up to the log. And you can tell he's ready. Ready to crunch down on you!

Don't scream yet. Turn to PAGE 43.

126

"Yay! Our hero!" the freaks cheer as they bolt out of their cells.

You follow the giant through a side exit. And in no time, you're leading all your new friends to your house.

You're sure your parents won't mind taking them in. After all, how much can a twenty stone giant, a thirty stone fat lady, and a three-headed man eat? Hmmmm. Better not answer that question.

Just be happy that you've come to . . .

THE END

You're not fast enough to get away from the ghost. You're running now, but the ghost swoops down in front of you. You plough into him—and pass right through him!

The carnival people are swarming after you. They don't want you to leave the carnival.

"Hurry!" you yell to your friends—only three minutes to midnight! You dash off in one direction, then another. The carnival people are approaching from every which way. They carry torches with flames that leap high in the air.

You steal a glance at your watch—11:58.

"We can't let them catch us!" you scream. "Let's hide!"

But where can you hide? Up ahead you see a gigantic cannon. All three of you could fit easily in there.

You also spot a baby ride—the baby choo-choo train—maybe you could squeeze into that.

Quick! Pick one—and hope for the best.

Cannon? Go to PAGE 130.
Choo-choo? Go to PAGE 128.

128

You squeeze into the choo-choo and scrunch down. 11:59.

Lights from the carnival people's torches sweep over you. Their foul smell fills your lungs.

The blood pounds in your temples.

You're sure they're going to find you. But you're trapped now.

There's no way out.

You hear someone shout in the distance. "Closing time!" And then you hear a bell start to chime . . .

. . . Midnight!

"One, two, three," Brad counts the chimes.

You want to strangle him!

"Four, five . . ."

Suddenly the kiddie train starts to move.

"Six . . . seven . . . eight . . ."

You sit up and what you see is the biggest shock of this whole horrible night . . .

Turn to PAGE 70.

The Monster Blood has grown so big—now you can't see over it or around it.

"Run for your lives!" Patty screams. But reaching the door is impossible.

The mound of green slime is bearing down on you. Fast! You stand frozen to the spot. Terrified. And then—just in time—you, Patty, and Brad leap to the side. And the Monster Blood slams into the wall with a crushing force—and ploughs right through it.

You stare at the giant gaping hole in the wall. Quickly, the three of you jump through the opening. You are standing outside the main gate—where you came in!

There's a wide path of destruction across the field and the forest beyond. From somewhere, a clock chimes twelve times, sending a chill down your spine. And when you peer back at the carnival, it has disappeared. All that's left is a spooky silver mist.

THE END

130

You and your friends squeeze into the cannon.

"Ouch! You're sitting on my hand," Brad whines.

But you don't have time to apologize.

"Do you smell something . . . burning?" you ask.

BOOM! There's a tremendous explosion. You fly through space. You are heading for a fence that encloses the carnival, and the field beyond.

Will you make it out of the park?

Go to PAGE 101.

SUCKER!

You didn't really think you could get out this easily, did you?

Check out the title of this book: *Escape From the Carnival of Horrors*.

Horrors! You need to face a lot more horrors— and then (maybe) you'll escape.

Quick! Turn to PAGE 116.

132

The fortune-teller said this number might save your life. But how?

Then you see it. In the corner. A tall silver locker with the number *132* painted in red.

"In here," you say, opening the door to the locker. You push Patty and Brad inside.

As soon as you close the door, the locker begins to rattle and shake. You're nearly blinded by a bright, white light. You hear a loud whooshing sound. And then all is silent. The door pops open—and you're amazed at what you see.

Turn to PAGE 21.

Those eyes behind the alligator snout—those beady eyes. You should have recognized them before. It's Big Al.

"Hey! You did a great job here," he says warmly. "You've really got the stuff for the Carnival of Horrors."

"Uh, thanks," you mumble. "But I really have to go home now."

"What's the rush?" he asks, patting you on the shoulder. "Aren't you having fun?"

Fun? you think. Crushed between solid walls. Then attacked by a bulging-eyed monster. Fun? No. This isn't fun. This is weird.

"Uh, yeah. It's been really great. But, um, I really do have to get home," you stammer. "So if you'll just take me to wherever Patty and Brad are—and show us the way out—we'll be going."

"I'm afraid that isn't possible," Big Al says. "Just open the door and you'll understand."

You have no choice. You have to open the door and go to PAGE 117.

134

You've got to figure out what you weigh on Mars. Fast. But how?

You're about to give up when you notice a flashing sign. It reads: THE GRAVITY ON MARS IS ALMOST 40 PERCENT OF WHAT IT IS ON EARTH. Okay, now you can figure it out.

Multiply your real Earth weight in pounds by four. (There are 14 pounds in a stone.) Now drop off the last digit. For example, if you weigh 90 pounds, 90 × 4 = 360. Dropping off the last digit, you get 36 for your weight on Mars.

If you don't want to do the maths, you can leave it to luck. Just guess.

If you think your Mars weight is 37 to 39, go to PAGE 53.

If you think your Mars weight is less than 37 or more than 39, go to PAGE 22.

You open the door and climb a steep ramp that curves round and round. It's cold and dark inside. Halfway up the ramp, you stop. There's another sign: WARNING!—YOU MAY BE THE ONE TO SLIDE TO YOUR DOOM!

You continue up the ramp. You finally make it to the top, and find yourself standing on a wide, dimly lit platform. A row of long, curving slides stretches out before you. The slides are numbered from one to ten.

You think hard. The Doom Slide. You know you've heard about it before. But where? Where was it?

And then you remember! It was in a GOOSE-BUMPS book you read! *One Day at HorrorLand*.

Now you know you're in big trouble. Because you remember all about the Doom Slide from the book. You remember that if you pick the wrong slide, you'll spend the rest of your life sliding and sliding—for ever!

Which number is the Doom Slide? Which one?

If you remember which number slide is the Doom Slide (or if you have the book and can look it up), choose a slide that is not the Doom Slide. If you can't remember, you'll have to leave it to luck. Pick a number between 1–10.

Pick slide 1, 4, or 5, and go to PAGE 121.
Pick slide 2, 7, or 9, and go to PAGE 95.
Pick slide 3, 6, 8, or 10, and go to PAGE 68.

R.L.Stine

Reader beware, you're in for a scare!
These terrifying tales will send shivers up your spine:

HIPPO FANTASY

Lose yourself in a whole new world, a world where anything is possible – from wizards and dragons, to time travel and new civilizations... Gripping, thrilling, scary and funny by turns, these Hippo Fantasy titles will hold you captivated to the very last page.

The Night of Wishes
Michael Ende

Malcolm and the Cloud-Stealer
Douglas Hill

The Crystal Keeper
James Jauncey

The Wednesday Wizard
Sherryl Jordan

Ratspell
Paddy Mounter

Rowan of Rin
Rowan and the Travellers
Emily Rodda

The Practical Princess
Jay Williams

The Babysitters Club

Need a babysitter? Then call the Babysitters Club. Kristy Thomas and her friends are all experienced sitters. They can tackle any job from rampaging toddlers to a pandemonium of pets. To find out all about them, read on!